For Fotis, my flame – S.P.C

For Adam, my match – S.H

JANETTA OTTER-BARRY BOOKS

Rama and Sita - Path of Flames copyright © Frances Lincoln Limited 2010
Text copyright © Sally Pomme Clayton 2010
Illustrations copyright © Sophie Herxheimer 2010

First published in Great Britain and in the USA in 2010 by
Frances Lincoln Children's Books, 4 Torriano Mews,
Torriano Avenue, London NW5 2RZ

www.franceslincoln.com

A catalogue record for this book is available from the British Library.

ISBN 978-1-84507-672-6

Illustrated with ink and collage
Set in Book Antiqua

Printed in Dongguan, Guangdong, China by Toppan Leefung in June 2010

1 3 5 7 9 8 6 4 2

Rama and Sita
Path of flames

TOLD BY
SALLY POMME CLAYTON

ILLUSTRATED BY
SOPHIE HERXHEIMER

F

FRANCES LINCOLN
CHILDREN'S BOOKS

CONTENTS

THE MONKEY

I like junk shops. Do you? I'm excited by tables piled with things that other people don't want! I hope that under the ragged clothes, old shoes and dusty books, I will find something beautiful, something special, something that needs to be taken home and kept.

Once, I did find something special. I found a monkey, a knitted monkey made from brown and orange wool. He was cheap. The lady behind the table pushed him, upside-down, into a plastic bag.

As soon as I was outside, I pulled the monkey out of the bag and examined him. He was a strange shape for a monkey – long and thin, with staring black eyes and ears that stuck out each side of his head – more like a teddy than a monkey. Then I noticed a little label on his leg that said *Made in China*.

"It's not true!" said a small voice.

I was looking round to see who had spoken, when the little voice spoke again.

"I wasn't made in China."

"Who said that?" I asked. "Did you speak, little monkey?"

"Don't call me little!" he cried.

"Sorry!" I said. "What shall I call you?"

"Hanuman."

I laughed. "Hanuman – the great Indian Monkey God – from the story of Rama and Sita?"

"Yep. That's me."

"But you can't be Hanuman. Your label says *Made in China*."

"Oh, that's because wherever I go, people think I belong to them. I was born in India. Then I got on a boat and crossed the sea to Indonesia. I did a bit of island hopping... Java... Bali. I travelled to the jungles of Vietnam, visited the temples of Cambodia, and on to the bustling streets of Singapore. I journeyed up into the mountains of China. And now I'm here – in Great Britain! And I belong to you."

"You've travelled a long way."

"I've been travelling for two thousand years. You see, I love the story of Rama and Sita, and whenever it's told, I'm there too, listening. It's a brilliant story, it's got magic and adventure, scary bits and funny bits – and I'm in it! You're going to be telling the story next, aren't you?"

"Well, yes," I mumbled. "My version of it."

"There can never be too many versions of this story," said Hanuman. "So get on with it... Begin!"

I carried Hanuman home and sat him above my desk. And that's where he is now, watching and listening, as I tell the story of Rama and Sita and their faithful friend, the monkey Hanuman.

HEAVEN TO EARTH

Through blue Heaven flew Garuda, King of the Birds. Giant Garuda with golden feathers soared across the sky, carrying Vishnu and Lakshmi on his back. Vishnu – God of Protection, and Lakshmi – Goddess of Love.

As Garuda swooped over Earth, Vishnu and Lakshmi looked down upon our world and saw flames. A path of flames. Houses were burning, people were running, children were crying. There were demons everywhere. The demons were stealing, fighting and making fires, greedily taking what wasn't theirs. The people on Earth were terrified. They hid in their homes in darkness, too afraid to go out, too afraid to light their lamps.

"What has happened to Earth?" cried Lakshmi.

"Demons are taking over," said Vishnu. "The Demon King, Ravana, wants to rule the world."

"We must do something," said Lakshmi.

"Yes," said Vishnu. "We must go down to Earth and stop him."

GRANTING WISHES

Once upon a time, in Northern India, there lived King Dasharatha, King of the West, and King Janaka, King of the East. The two kings lived in luxury. They each had a palace made of marble and treasure houses filled with jewels. They wore robes of silk and sat on couches embroidered with gold. They had armies of elephants and retinues of servants. They sipped cool drinks, ate dishes of spicy rice and sticky sweets made of honey whenever they wished. They wandered through gardens of jasmine, rested on shady verandahs and listened to splashing fountains.

Each king had a beautiful queen. But neither king was happy. They had everything, everything except children. The kings wished, hoped and prayed for children. They waited and waited. But no children came.

Then Dasharatha, King of the West, had an idea: he took two more wives. He had two enormous weddings. He now had three queens – but still no children came.

So King Dasharatha went to the temple to pray. He made an offering to Agni, the God of Fire, placing his hands together, bending his head and bowing solemnly to the flames.

"*Om Agni swaha*," he prayed. "Agni, God of Fire, I salute you! Bring light into my life. Bring me a child."

Suddenly the fire burned brightly. King Dasharatha stared at the fire, and the flames glittered and danced into the shape of a tiger. The flames flashed and became a blazing eye, flickered into a brilliant burning hand, then took the form of a red mouth, opening and closing. The fiery hand reached towards the king and held out a shining bowl.

The fiery mouth whispered, "Eat and be happy."

Then the flames went out and there, standing in the ashes, was the shining bowl. King Dasharatha thanked Agni, bent down and picked up the bowl. Inside were three luscious pieces of fruit.

The king smiled. "One for each of my queens!" he said.

As each queen ate a fruit, happiness filled her heart. A few weeks passed, and each queen knew she would have a child. Nine months later, King Dasharatha became a father. His wish had been granted, not just once, but four times. His three queens gave birth to four baby boys: Rama, Bharata, and the twins, Shatrughna and Lakshman. The King of the West was no longer sad, he had four handsome sons!

When King Janaka, the King of the East, heard about the miracle of the flames, he went to his temple early one morning and made an offering to the sacred fire.

"*Om Agni swaha*, bring me a child."

The king watched the fire. But nothing happened. The flames did not glitter or dance. There was no fiery hand or burning bowl. There was no miracle for him.

King Janaka was sad. He went out into his garden, but even the beauty of the trees and the scent of jasmine could not lift his heart.

Then he heard crying. The king looked about, but it was early and the garden was still empty. The crying grew louder and louder. 'It sounds just like a baby,' thought the king. He walked towards the sound – it seemed to be coming from underground. King Janaka knelt down and began to dig in the earth with his bare hands. He turned over the furrows and saw a tiny face and little hands. Buried in the brown earth was a baby!

The king carefully scraped back the soil and the baby wriggled. It was a little girl. He gently lifted her out of the ground and hugged her tight. She was beautiful, with dark eyes and black hair.

Joy filled the king's heart and, holding the baby close, he carried her to the palace. "Wishes are granted in unexpected ways," King Janaka said to his queen. "At last we have a child."

King Janaka and his queen loved the baby as if it was their own. And they called her Sita, which means furrow, because they had found her in the brown earth.

BREAKING THE BOW

The whole palace loved Sita. As soon as she could walk, she was given the freedom to go wherever she wanted. She ran through the chambers and banqueting halls and out into the gardens, making friends with everyone. The servants let her do things no one else was allowed to do. They gave her rides on the elephants, they let her bathe in the fountains and climb the biggest trees in the garden. No one was sure if it was real or an illusion, but wherever Sita walked, plants seemed to lean towards her and flowers burst into blossom.

Sita grew into a young woman. Her dark hair reached her waist, swinging and shining as she walked. She stood straight and strong as a tree, moving gracefully, like a reed bending in the breeze. When she giggled, it sounded like a tinkling stream, and her hands danced like fluttering leaves. Sita was as beautiful as the earth from which she had been born.

News spread of Sita's beauty, and soon King Janaka was overwhelmed with requests for his daughter's hand in marriage.

One day, as the king was walking with his daughter through the garden, he pointed to a patch of earth beneath a tree.

"That is the happy place where I found you," he said. "It seems like yesterday. I can hardly believe that the light of my life has grown into such a beautiful young woman. You are so special, Sita, I don't know how to choose the right husband for you."

Sita caught her father's arm.

"Papa, I've been reading the ancient stories, and in the old days, princesses made up their own minds about who they would marry."

"That is true," said the king. "They would hold a *swayamvara* – a contest.

11

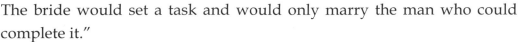

The bride would set a task and would only marry the man who could complete it."

"Oh! Let's do the same, Papa," cried Sita. "And let the test be this: I will only marry the man who can lift Shiva's golden bow."

"But that is impossible!" said King Janaka. "That bow was left on Earth by Shiva – God of Creation and Destruction. The bow is so enormous, no human being could ever lift it."

Sita's eyes twinkled. "Well then, if someone manages to lift Shiva's bow, we will know they are special."

Her father nodded his head in agreement.

News travelled to kingdoms near and far: there was going to be a competition for Sita's hand in marriage. Soon there was a long queue of suitors standing outside the palace gates – princes and farmers, soldiers and artists, teachers and craftsmen – and they all wanted to marry Sita.

The day of the contest arrived and the palace gates were thrown open.

"Welcome," said King Janaka, "to Sita's *swayamvara*."

The suitors crowded into the banqueting hall and the king commanded, "Bring out the bow!"

Five thousand soldiers took their places along lengths of thick, heavy rope. "PUUUULLLLLLL!" shouted their captain. The soldiers hauled at the ropes, tugging and pulling, until the whole palace began to shake. They dragged a massive cart into the hall, a cart that was so big, it had a hundred wheels. But the cart was nothing compared to what it was carrying. On it lay an enormous, shining bow. The bow was so vast, it looked like an arching bridge, big enough to span a river. It was Shiva's bow, and it was made of pure gold.

Sita stood beside her father, holding a garland of flowers. She raised her garland in the air, and the king shouted, "Let the competition begin!"

A prince wearing a turban covered in jewels with a large feather bobbing on the top, stepped forward. He bowed grandly and the feather bowed too.

"A princess should wed a prince," he said. "And I am honoured to lift the bow for you." He blew Sita a kiss, then delicately placed his fingers on the bow. He bent to lift the bow, and tumbled to the ground.

"It's not fair!" complained the prince, rubbing his bruises. "This task is impossible."

But Sita's father did not have time to waste discussing the matter. "Next!" he shouted.

A soldier stepped forward, turning this way and that, making sure that the whole court could see how broad his chest was.

"I work with weapons, Princess. I know all about bows and arrows." He knelt down, clutched the bow tightly with his fists, and using all his might, tried to lift it. He heaved, and heaved, and heaved, and heaved….

"Next!" cried the king.

A farmer stepped forward, rubbing the dirt from his large hands.

"My lady, I work in the fields all day, I know about lifting things." He curled his thick fingers under the bow and gripped hard. Straining and groaning, he used all his power, but he could not budge the bow.

"Next!" yawned the king.

One by one, the suitors tried. And one by one, they failed. The bow was too heavy to lift. The king turned to Sita and shook his head. It seemed that no one was special enough to marry his daughter.

'How sad,' he thought, 'she will remain alone all her life.'

The garland of flowers hung loose in Sita's hand.

Suddenly two young men pushed through the crowd.

"I am Prince Rama," said a tall, noble-looking man, "and this is my youngest brother, Prince Lakshman. We have journeyed from the Kingdom of the West. We are sons of King Dasharatha." Rama placed his hands together. "I would like to lift the bow."

Sita gazed at Rama. His face was radiant, and very handsome. 'What a shame,' she thought, 'that this task is impossible.'

Rama bent and lightly grasped the bow. Then, gently, he began to lift it, as if he were plucking a flower. He lifted the bow up and up, above his head, high into the air. The whole palace gasped. Then Rama began to bend the bow. Everyone stared in amazement. Suddenly there was a loud crack, and the bow snapped in two. Rama had broken Shiva's bow! And the sound echoed across the world.

Sita lifted the garland of flowers and placed it around Rama's neck.

"I don't know if you are a human or a god, a lion or a man," she laughed. "But I am so glad that it was you who lifted the bow."

And so there was a wedding, with feasting and dancing, music and storytelling. It went on for days and days. And the whole world was so happy, it rained flowers.

After the wedding, a procession of elephants left the Kingdom of the East, carrying Rama, Sita, and Lakshman to the Kingdom of the West.

But deep in the forest, Ravana, King of the Demons, heard the bow snap, and he began to make a plan.

KEEPING PROMISES

Cheering crowds surrounded Rama and his party as they arrived in the Kingdom of the West. Musicians played drums, and people scattered rice and flowers to bless the new bride. Rama's brothers, Bharata and Shatrughna, pushed through the crowds to meet them.

"Welcome, Sita!" the brothers said, bowing low. "Welcome, sister, to your new home."

Sita smiled and returned the bow.

"Let's show you the palace," said Bharata.

"And the gardens," said Shatrughna.

"And you must meet Father!" they both cried.

Sita laughed. She knew she would be happy here.

When at last Rama and Sita sat in the shade, drinking tea with all the family, the whole palace seemed to glow with happiness. Only Bharata's mother, the second queen, did not join in the party.

King Dasharatha closed his eyes and thought, 'It is time for me to pass on the throne. It is time for me to let my son take over.' Dasharatha smiled to himself. 'Rama is the eldest and he is married now. He will make an excellent king.'

But even in this peaceful moment, Ravana's demons were moving, gathering in the distance.

A few days later, King Dasharatha called a family meeting. He welcomed his three queens, four sons, and new daughter Sita with trays of sweets and cool drinks.

"My family," said the king. "I have an announcement to make. I have decided that the time has come for my eldest son Rama to take the throne. Rama will be King."

The brothers rushed to embrace Rama. But Bharata's mother stepped forward. "My husband, do you remember that you promised me two wishes on my wedding day?"

King Dasharatha nodded.

"I have never used my wishes."

"What is it you wish for?" said the king, taking the queen's hands in his.

"My first wish is for my son, Bharata, to be king. And my second wish is for Rama to be banished to the forest."

King Dasharatha was horrified. "My queen, ask for something else, I implore you. You can have anything, anything, but this."

"You promised to grant my wishes," said the queen.

Bharata turned to his mother.

"Has a demon got into your mind?" he cried. "This is wrong, Mother. Rama is the eldest son. He must take Father's place and become king."

Bharata's mother glared. "A king should keep his promises."

"That is true," said Bharata, "but these are the wishes of the Devil."

King Dasharatha shook his head sadly. How quickly peace had been disrupted by dispute.

"Silence, Bharata," he said. Then he looked solemnly at his wife.

"Your requests break my heart. But I promised you two wishes, and you shall have them. Bharata will be King. Rama will be banished."

16

For a moment the whole kingdom fell silent, and then a storm erupted as everyone began to weep and wail. Everyone except Rama. He bent his head and bowed respectfully to his father. Then he went to his rooms and prepared to leave, taking off his silken robes and putting on the rough clothes of exile.

Sita watched him pack a few belongings into an old bag. "I'm coming with you," she said.

Rama shook his head. "I am banished to the forest, Sita. There will be no palace or servants. I will have trees for my roof and leaves for my carpet. And it will be dangerous. The forest is full of demons."

Sita wept. "This palace will be worse than a forest, and loneliness will be more terrifying than demons if I am without you. Please let me come."

"I agree with Sita," said Lakshman, bursting into the room. "She can't stay here. And neither can I. I'm coming too – and don't even think about arguing."

And so Rama, Sita and Lakshman turned their backs on the palace and walked towards the forest. The King of the West watched them go, with tears running down his cheeks.

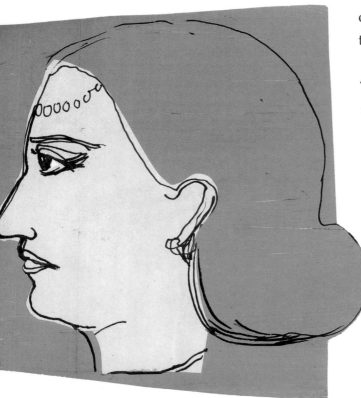

But Bharata rushed after them. "Rama!" he called. "Give me your sandals. I will place them on the throne to remind everyone that the throne really belongs to you, and that I am only taking care of the kingdom until you return."

Rama bent down, took off his sandals and pressed them into his brother's hands.

"If we return," he said.

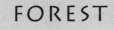

DEMONS IN THE TREES

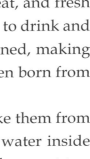

Rama, Sita and Lakshman entered the forest. It was dark and cold. Rama marched grimly ahead. This was not the future he wanted for his wife – to live in poverty and exile in a forest.

But as Sita walked, branches and bushes moved aside, allowing them to pass. Juicy berries ripened, beckoning them to pick and eat, and fresh springs of water gushed up from underground, calling them to drink and bathe. They made a camp, and trees bent low, leaves entwined, making a soft green canopy for them to shelter beneath. Sita had been born from the earth, and Earth took care of her child.

The forest became their home. Every morning, birds woke them from their beds of grass. Lakshman made a fire, and Sita boiled water inside a hollowed–out rock, adding flower petals and herbs to make sweet tea. They found picnic spots and bathing places, and during the hot afternoons they would rest in the shade, listening to the hum of crickets. Sita spoke to all the animals and birds, and made friends with a large vulture – the wise and kind Jatayu.

"Be careful, my friends," cawed the vulture. "The forest is full of demons. I will watch from above during the day, but you must keep a fire burning at night."

Jatayu kept his promise to protect them. He spread his great wings and soared above the trees, circling overhead, keeping a sharp look–out for anything dangerous. And at night Lakshman built up the fire, and they took it in turns to stay awake and keep watch.

Hiding in the trees were demons, demons everywhere, spying on Rama and Sita. The demons hid in the branches and peered through the leaves, their eyes glinting in the dark, greedily waiting for the fire to go out, waiting for the moment to pounce.

"Hush, my demons," whispered Ravana, their king. "We must take care. The treasure is a great one. We don't want to rush in and lose it."

Ravana, with ten heads, twenty arms, twenty red eyes and ten long black tongues, watched Sita. 'Sita is the jewel of jewels,' he thought. 'I must have her.'

He called for his servant, and the demon Maricha appeared. He had red horns, red hooves, a red tail and evil red eyes.

"You called, Your Honour?" he said, bowing low.

"I am on fire, Maricha!" cried Ravana.

"Shall I put it out?" asked Maricha, stamping the ground with his hooves.

"Certainly not, you fool!" shouted Ravana. "This is the fire of love. I am in love with Sita. She is beauty itself. I want Sita. And what I want, I get. Maricha, you must disguise yourself. I don't care how, but do it. Tempt Rama and Lakshman away from Sita. Then, when Sita is alone, I will capture her. She will be mine!"

THE GOLDEN DEER

One morning, Sita saw a flash of gold between the trees. She gazed into the forest, thinking it must be sunlight dancing on the leaves. But the flash of gold came closer, darting this way and that. Out of the trees bounded a little deer. A little deer made entirely of gold.

Sita gasped. "Rama!" she cried. "Come quickly! Look at this creature. It's a deer with a golden coat! If only I could have it as a pet."

Rama and Lakshman stood beside Sita and watched the deer lift its golden head, its eyes blazing like jewels.

"Of course you may have the creature, my darling," said Rama. "I will catch it for you."

"Wait, brother!" said Lakshman. "It could be a trick."

"How could it possibly be a trick?" asked Sita. "It's so sweet!"

The deer began leaping and jumping, its coat sparkling.

"Deer are not made of gold," said Lakshman firmly. "It might be magic."

Rama turned to his brother.

"Lakshman, would you deny Sita this small pleasure? She has followed me faithfully into the forest, and she has nothing. Let me give her this one gift."

There was a flash of gold, and the deer bounded off between the trees.

"Catch it for me, Rama!" cried Sita.

Lakshman shook his head. "Don't go, brother – it's dangerous."

But Rama pulled a rope from his bag and said, "Take care of Sita while I'm gone. And whatever you do, Lakshman, don't leave her."

Rama ran through the forest, chasing the golden deer. The deer was swift, but Rama was a good hunter. He coiled the rope into a noose and whirled it above his head, to lasso the creature. Suddenly the deer stopped running away from Rama. It turned, and started running towards him. The deer roared. Its eyes turned red. Red horns pushed out of its golden head, red hooves appeared on its golden feet. The deer turned into a demon, the demon Maricha!

Maricha grinned, and shouted in a voice that sounded just like Rama's. "Help me, brother! Help me!"

On the other side of the forest, Sita heard Rama's cry.

"Oh, Lakshman, did you hear that? Rama is in trouble. You must help him."

Lakshman shook his head. "Rama made me promise not to leave you," he said.

The cry came again, echoing across the forest. "Brother! Help me!"

"Please go," begged Sita. "Rama needs you."

Lakshman stood still for a moment, listening to Rama's voice calling through the trees.

"Very well, I'll go. But I am not happy about it." He bent down and picked up a large stone and began to draw a circle in the dust – a circle around Sita.

"This is a magic circle," he said. "It will protect you until we return. Whatever you do, don't step out of the circle."

And Lakshman ran off after his brother.

THE MAGIC CIRCLE

Sita stood alone in the centre of the magic circle and waited.

The sun vanished behind a cloud. And suddenly, Sita heard a voice calling, "Food, I beg you. Food for a hungry man." And an old man dressed in rags, holding an empty wooden bowl, stumbled through the trees.

Sita bowed. He must be a holy man, she thought, wandering from place to place, begging for food.

The old man held out his bowl. "Food for a traveller."

"Good sir," said Sita. "I am unable to feed you today."

The old man touched trembling fingers to his lips. "Please, lady, I haven't eaten for a week."

"I am sorry, holy Father, I wish I could help, but I mustn't step out of this circle."

The old man hobbled closer. "I haven't drunk for days," he begged. "Just a sip of water."

"Oh, poor man," said Sita, moving to the edge of the magic circle. "I know it is my duty to feed you, but I promised not to leave the circle."

"I am a holy man," said the old man, holding out his hand. "No harm will come to you. Here, take my hand."

Sita stretched out her hand and the old man grasped it.

"Thank you, lady, I knew you would come to my aid."

Sita held the old man's hand and he helped her step out of the magic circle. He clutched Sita's hand tight and pulled her close. There was a brilliant flash of light, and out of the old man's body burst ten heads, twenty arms, twenty red eyes, and ten black tongues. The old man turned into Ravana, the Demon King.

Ravana seized Sita in his twenty arms, and the ten heads cried, "Now you're mine! I will take you to Lanka, the Demon Kingdom, and you will be my queen."

"I don't want to be your queen!" cried Sita.

"Oh, you'll change your mind," laughed Ravana, "when you see all my gold and jewels."

Ravana muttered magic words and a golden chariot appeared. He pulled Sita inside and cried, "To the Demon Kingdom, my chariot!"

Instantly the magic chariot rose up into the air. The golden chariot rose higher and higher into the sky. Sita screamed for help, but her cries were blown away by the wind. Desperately she clutched at her golden necklace, tore it off, and hurled it to the ground in the hope that Rama might find it and save her.

THE WOUNDED VULTURE

Jatayu, the wise vulture, was circling above the trees when he spotted Ravana's chariot speeding away. Beautiful Sita was trapped inside. Jatayu flew after the chariot. He spread his great wings wide, flapped them hard, and blew up a storm. He beat his wings and wind buffeted the chariot, rocking it from side to side.

"Let Sita go!" he cawed, swooping low over the chariot.

"Out of my way, you ugly bird!" shouted Ravana, beating Jatayu with his twenty arms.

Sita clung to the side of the chariot. "Help me, Jatayu. Save me!" she sobbed.

Jatayu dived at the chariot, pecking and clawing Ravana.

"Ridiculous creature!" laughed Ravana, pulling a ten–sided sword from his belt. With one swipe of the sword, Ravana slashed Jatayu's wings, cutting the feathers. The vulture plunged to the ground.

"My beloved Jatayu!" cried Sita.

Ravana calmly wiped the sword. "Home, chariot. Take me and my queen home." The magic chariot rose higher and turned towards Lanka.

"You can carry me away," wept Sita, "but you will never make me your queen."

All this time, Rama and Lakshman had been fighting the demon Maricha. At last, they won the fight. The demon was dead. The brothers raced back to camp and found the magic circle empty. They called for Sita, but there was no reply. They looked everywhere, but Sita had gone.

Then Rama saw something glittering on the ground. It was Sita's golden necklace. He bent and picked it up.

"Something terrible has happened," he said. "We must find Sita."

The brothers set off. They had not gone far when they saw spots of blood on the ground. They followed the trail of blood through the trees, and found Jatayu, lying in a pool of blood, with both his wings cut. Rama and Lakshman knelt beside the vulture.

"What happened?" asked Rama.

Jatayu had little breath left. "Ravana… stolen… Sita…" he croaked.

"Where?" begged the brothers.

But Jatayu had breathed his last breath, and before he could answer, he was dead.

The brothers embraced the bird. "Oh, faithful friend," said Rama, "you gave your life protecting us."

"We will remember your courage and release your soul," said Lakshman.

Lakshman collected branches and twigs and made a fire. And they held a funeral for Jatayu. They placed his body in the red flames, and wept blue tears. They sang the life and death of the noble bird. White smoke curled into the sky, carrying Jatayu's soul to heaven, where he was reunited with his father, Garuda, for all eternity.

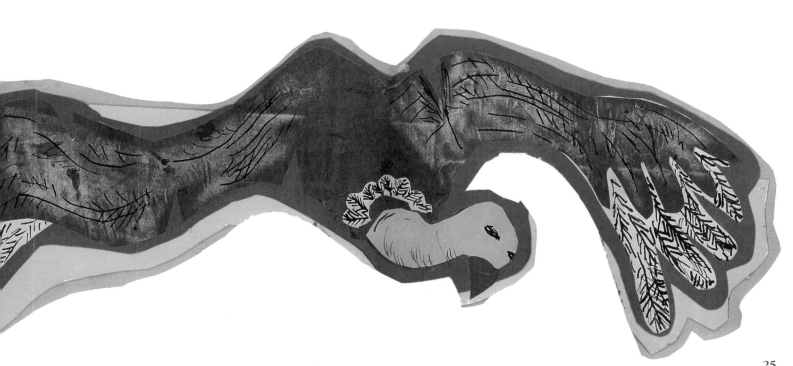

THE MONKEY KINGDOM

"South," said Rama, "to Ravana's kingdom."

The brothers walked all day. They scrambled through forests and crossed rivers. They pushed their way through tangled jungles, clambered up stony paths and jumped over streams, on the quest for the Demon Kingdom.

The brothers walked south and south, until they came to wild mountains. They heard a chattering sound.

"There seem to be a lot of monkeys here," said Lakshman, looking about. There were monkeys everywhere, hanging from trees, perched on rocks and crouched under bushes. The monkeys saw Rama and Lakshman and erupted into loud screeching. Then, leaping and running, squealing and shrieking, they surrounded the brothers and began poking and prodding them.

"Handsome lads, aren't they!" grinned one monkey.

"Too tall!" teased another.

"Not much hair!" yelled a third.

A monkey jumped on to Lakshman's shoulder, "Nice teeth!" he chattered.

The monkeys swarmed over the brothers.

"STOP!" cried Rama. "That's enough. Now, monkeys, do you know where Lanka is?"

A strange silence fell, and a small brown monkey hopped forward. "Why would you want to go there?" he asked in a tiny voice.

"Ravana has stolen Sita," said Rama.

"Not beautiful, kind Sita?" said the littlest monkey. "Follow me – you need the help of our king."

The monkey led Rama and Lakshman over the mountain, to a glade of trees.

"Welcome to the Monkey Kingdom!" he said. Then, in the grandest voice he could find, the little monkey announced, "His Royal Highness, Sugreeva, King of the Monkeys."

Sitting on a banana throne, wearing a banana crown, leaning on a banana table and eating three bananas, was a giant monkey with silver fur. Rama and Lakshman bowed low. The king took one of the bananas out of his mouth and mumbled, "Refreshments for the visitors!"

At once, Rama and Lakshman were given banana leaf plates piled high with sweet bananas. The brothers were starving after their long journey and gobbled up the fruit. Monkeys clambered into the trees and tore down large coconuts, and the brothers gulped the sweet, refreshing, coconut milk.

"Nothing like a good meal to prepare you for a meeting," said King Sugreeva. "Now, tell me your story."

Rama began. "Ravana has stolen Sita, and we must get her back."

"What?" cried the Monkey King. "Not beautiful, kind Sita?" The monkeys chattered loudly.

"Quiet!" commanded Sugreeva. "Ravana is dangerous," he continued. "Very dangerous. And he's clever."

"That's because he has ten heads!" cried the monkeys.

"Silence!" shouted Sugreeva. Then he looked sternly at Rama and Lakshman. "You can't go to Lanka alone. You need protection. My monkeys will go with you. They will be your army. And, Hanuman, you will be the General."

The littlest monkey stepped forward and bowed. "Hanuman, at your service. I will do everything I can to save Sita."

"You?" smiled Rama. "You are the leader?"

He chuckled, and the chuckle turned into a big belly laugh. "You can't possibly be General – you're too little!"

The monkey screwed up his face. "Don't call me little," he said in his loudest voice. And he began to grow. Bigger, and bigger, and bigger. He grew to the size of a normal monkey. He grew to the size of a king monkey. He grew to the size of a human being. He grew to the size of an elephant. He grew to the size of the tallest tree. Rama looked up, and up, and up, and the littlest monkey towered above him.

"Forgive me!" cried Rama. "You MUST be the leader."

And so Rama, Lakshman and the monkeys set off, with Hanuman in front as General.

Jai, jai, jai, Hanuman Gosai,
kripa karahu,
gurudev ki naee.

Hail, hail, hail, Lord Hanuman,
bless us, teach us, protect us,
oh great God.

THE MONKEYS GO SOUTH

The band of monkeys trooped south, towards Lanka. They walked all day and late into the night, singing to keep their spirits up. When Rama or Lakshman grew tired, Hanuman picked them up and carried them on his shoulders.

They entered a thick forest, and had not gone far when they heard a loud snoring sound. The band stopped and listened – the whole forest seemed to be snuffling, grunting, and snoring!

"Keep quiet!" whispered Hanuman. "This is the Bear Kingdom. Bears love to sleep. We must walk carefully so we don't wake them."

The band crept as quietly as they could through the forest. The monkeys lifted their paws gently and placed them down softly on the ground. Rama lifted his foot and brought it down CRACK! on a twig. The sound echoed through the trees.

There was a giant roar.

"WHO DARES WAKE ME UP?"

Out of the undergrowth lumbered an enormous black bear.

"Quick!" whispered Hanuman. "Bow! It's Jambuvan, King of the Bears."

"Is that you, Hanuman?" growled the black bear. "Are you stealing berries?"

"Certainly not, Your Majesty. Ravana has stolen Sita and I'm leading an army to Lanka to get her back."

Jambuvan was suddenly awake. His huge black head swayed from side to side and his eyes flashed.

"Sita, daughter of Earth, stolen? We bears knew something was wrong. We saw plants and flowers dying, but did not know why. Now I understand. Mother Earth is crying for her daughter, and she will go on crying until Sita is set free."

Jambuvan stood up on his hind legs, threw back his giant head and roared, "BEARS! AWAKE!"

There were groans and grumbles as the bears woke up. They stumbled out of caves, from beneath bushes and under trees, until the whole forest was alive with bears.

"Let's join the monkey band!" cried Jambuvan.

And so Rama and Lakshman, Hanuman and Jambuvan, the monkeys and the bears, travelled south. And south. And south.

"Are we there yet?" asked Lakshman.

"Can't be far now," said Hanuman.

The land became flatter and flatter. Brown earth turned to yellow sand. And they came to the edge of the sea. Stretching into the distance was a vast ocean.

Rama looked this way and that. "Where's Lanka?" he said. "Where is the Demon Kingdom?"

All he could see was water – endless blue water.

SITA CAPTIVE

All this time, Sita was a prisoner on the island of Lanka, far over the sea. In the centre of Lanka was a fortress made of thick, impenetrable stone. It had soaring towers and hidden battlements, where demons kept guard night and day. Inside the fortress was Ravana's palace, built from everything the demons had stolen. The walls were made of gold and the floors of silver. There were fountains and pools, and the furniture was studded with the rarest jewels.

Although Sita was a captive, she was treated like a queen. Demons brought her trays piled with ripe mango, coconut pancakes topped with palm tree syrup and glasses of cool pineapple juice. But Sita refused to eat, and as the weeks passed she grew thinner and paler.

Each day, Ravana visited her, bowed politely, and gave her presents – a jade necklace, a silk dress, a ruby ring. But Sita refused all of them.

"Take them," said Ravana. "I am burning up with love for you, Sita!"

"Burn away," murmured Sita.

Ravana spread his twenty arms wide and said, "Marry me, Sita. This palace, and all that is in it, will be yours."

Sita closed her eyes and said, "I am already married, to Rama."

"But he's lost to you now," shouted Ravana. "You are here with me, for ever. And if you won't marry me, I will kill you. Do you hear? You have one month to make up your mind. Marry me, or die."

REMEMBER WHO YOU ARE

Hanuman looked out across the endless blue ocean.

"Lanka must be somewhere over there," he said. "But how are we going to get across all this water?"

The monkeys and bears shook their heads, and Rama and Lakshman sat in silence, too downhearted to speak.

Then Jambuvan, King of the Bears, turned to Hanuman.

"My friend," he said, "you will have to leap to Lanka."

"What!" cried Hanuman. "Jump over the sea? That's impossible."

"You're a good jumper," said Jambuvan.

"And you're joking," said Hanuman.

Jambuvan shook his furry head. "Why would I joke?"

"Because it's a ridiculous idea."

Jambuvan looked sternly at the little monkey.

"Of course you can leap to Lanka!" he said. "Remember who you are. You are Hanuman, son of the wind. Your father is Vyu – God of the Wind. You have your father's strength and power. Like the wind, Hanuman, you can change your shape. You can become smaller than a mouse and slip through a key–hole. You can grow bigger than a giant and fill a great hall. And even when you were a tiny baby, you loved to jump!"

Hanuman smiled and Jambuvan nodded his head. "Don't you remember, Hanuman? Once, when you were very young, you saw the sun shining in the sky and thought it was a rubber ball."

Hanuman chuckled.

"You jumped into the sky and tried to catch the sun. You jumped, and jumped, and jumped. You jumped so high, you nearly touched the sun. You jumped so high, you burned yourself, and your fur has been brown ever since!"

Hanuman laughed.

And Jambuvan continued, "Surya the Sun God was impressed. He was amazed that you had jumped so high, and he gave you a gift – the gift of immortality. So, like the sun, you will never die. Like the sun, you will live for ever. Remember who you are, Hanuman, and leap to Lanka."

Hanuman looked out at the vast, endless ocean. "I will try," he said.

The monkeys and the bears cheered.

Rama stepped forward, pulling a jewelled ring from his finger.

"My General," he said. "If you see Sita, give her my ring. Tell her I love her and will save her."

Hanuman put the ring into his furry pocket and turned to face the sea.

HANUMAN'S LEAP

Hanuman pressed his paws together and prayed, "Father Wind, help me now."

Then he bent his knees, lengthened his tail, opened his arms, and jumped with all his might. The wind caught him and lifted him up. Hanuman leapt higher and higher. He hurtled through the air.

"Go! Hanuman, go!" shouted the monkeys and the bears, as Hanuman leapt up and up, and disappeared into the blue sky.

Hanuman leapt over shimmering blue sea, under wide blue sky. Swifter than a bird, swifter than thought, Hanuman flew!

The ocean rumbled, and a great rock rose out of the sea.

"Rest, son of Vyu," called the rock. "I am a friend of your father's. Come and rest here."

But Hanuman hurtled past the rock. "Sorry!" he shouted. "Can't stop!"

The rock sank down under the waves, calling, "Be careful. There are demons everywhere."

Then Hanuman saw something glittering in the sea, far, far, below. Shaped like a teardrop and gleaming like a jewel – it was Lanka!

Hanuman leapt, swifter than a hurricane, swifter than a tornado. He was nearly there.

Suddenly the sky grew dark. A huge demon with vast wings blocked Hanuman's path. It lashed a long black tail and snapped open its huge red jaws.

"No one enters Lanka without entering my mouth first!" the demon roared.

Hanuman felt himself being sucked into the demon's dark mouth. There was no escape.

Then Hanuman heard a voice whispering in his head, "Remember who you are."

Instantly Hanuman knew what to do. He changed his shape. He shrank to the size of a mosquito and buzzed into the demon's mouth. And before the demon could close its jaws, Hanuman buzzed out again.

"I've entered your mouth," cried Hanuman. "And now I'll enter Lanka!"

Hanuman leapt, swifter than light, swifter than the blink of an eye. He circled over the island, swooped down and landed on the shores of the Demon Kingdom.

SITA'S PLEA

Hanuman shrank to the size of a mouse and scurried through Lanka. He scampered under golden doors, over silver floors, in and out of houses, halls and bedrooms, looking for Sita.

There were demons everywhere, eating, drinking and playing cards. Hanuman crept past demons with green tongues and yellow fangs, with heads of donkeys and bodies of snakes, bulging eyes and dangling noses, feet that turned backwards and mouths in their bellies. Hanuman sneaked past dancing demons, storytelling demons and snoring demons. There were lots and lots of demons, but no Sita.

Then Hanuman heard sobbing. He followed the sound to a little garden. And there, sitting under a tree, was a girl. She was as beautiful as the Earth, with dark eyes and black hair, but she was pale and thin, and she was weeping. A gaggle of hideous demonesses crowded round her.

One demoness prodded Sita with a fat green finger. "What a fool you are," she shrieked. "Marry Ravana – you'll be rich."

"You'll be dead if you don't!" cackled another demoness, poking Sita in the ribs.

"Bet your liver is tender," cried a third demoness, flicking a long black tongue out of her mouth. "I'd like to gobble you up!"

Quickly Hanuman climbed the tree and dropped the ring into Sita's lap.

Sita gasped. It was Rama's ring! She looked up, and there was a little monkey hiding in the branches. Hanuman winked and put his paw to his lips.

"Sssshh!" he whispered.

Sita hid the ring in the folds of her dress.

"Rama loves you," whispered Hanuman. "He will save you."

"Tell him to hurry," Sita begged. "I only have three more weeks to live."

"What's she going on about?" said one of the demonesses.

"Oi!" said a second. "Who's she talking to?"

"It's that monkey in the tree," cried a third.

"Oooo, monkeys can't come to Lanka without a passport," they all screeched. "They might bring diseases."

And before Hanuman could shrink or grow, run or fly, the demonesses screamed, "Grab him!" Then they caught him in their fat hands, squeezed him tight, and carried him to Ravana.

HANUMAN ON FIRE

"What have we here?" roared Ravana. "A spying little monkey?"

"Don't call me little," muttered Hanuman.

Ravana sneered, and paraded Hanuman before his army of demons. "What shall we do with him, demons? Any ideas?"

The demons giggled. "Monkeys love their tails, they do!" They burst into shrieks of laughter. "Set fire to his tail!"

"Good idea!" said Ravana. "Wrap his tail in cotton, soak it in oil, and then we'll watch him burn."

The demons jumped about in excitement. "What fun!" they cried.

A cotton sheet and a jar of oil was brought into Ravana's banqueting hall. The demons began to wrap strips of cotton around Hanuman's tail and to soak the cotton in oil. But Hanuman knew what to do. He made his tail grow. The demons carried on wrapping and soaking, but Hanuman's tail grew longer and longer.

"More cotton! More oil!" shouted the demons. Bales of cotton and barrels of oil were dragged into the hall. The demons wrapped and soaked, soaked and wrapped, but they could not reach the end of Hanuman's tail. Hanuman's tail just grew longer, and longer, and longer – until the demons ran out of cotton and oil.

"Oh! Just set fire to his tail anyway!" shouted Ravana.

The demons took a burning torch, lit the end of Hanuman's tail, and stood back to watch.

As Hanuman's tail began to burn, he shrank to the size of a mouse. Hanuman's tail shrank too. The cloth unravelled all over the floor and the floor began to burn.

The demons started shouting, and rushed around trying to put the fire out.

Hanuman leapt on to Ravana's throne. The tip of his tail was still alight, and the throne of jewels burst into flames. The demons began calling for water and furiously beat back the fire. And in the smoke and flames and chaos, Hanuman escaped.

Hanuman leapt through Lanka, jumping from roof-top to roof-top, leaving behind a path of flames. When he reached the seashore, he dipped the tip of his tail into the sea and put out the flames.

"Ah!" he sighed. "That's better." Then Hanuman pressed his paws together and prayed. "Father Wind, help me now."

He bent his knees, lengthened his tail, opened his arms and jumped. He hurtled through the air. Swifter than a bird, swifter than thought. Swifter than a hurricane, swifter than a tornado. Swifter than light, swifter than the blink of an eye.

The rock rose from the ocean, offering him a place of rest. But Hanuman flew on, until he saw Jambuvan waving, and Rama running across the beach to greet him.

BUILDING A BRIDGE

"Sita is alive!" cried Hanuman. "But we have to be quick. We must get to Lanka before Ravana kills her."

Rama clutched his bow. "How will we cross the sea?" he said.

Jambuvan stepped forward. "We'll build a bridge."

The monkeys and bears gathered stones and began throwing them into the water, but the stones spiralled down to the bottom of the sea. The monkeys hurled rocks into the ocean, but they sank down to the sea–bed. The bears pulled up trees by their roots and threw them into the ocean, but the trees floated away on the tide. They worked all day, but there was nothing to show for their labour. There was no bridge. There wasn't even a jetty.

The monkeys and bears collapsed on the sand. "We'll never build a bridge to Lanka," they sighed.

Just then, the surface of the sea began to bubble. The sea glittered and the water frothed and foamed.

"Look!" cried Lakshman. "Look at all those fish."

The monkeys and bears sat up and looked out to sea. The water was filled with fish. There were silvery eels and big fat tuna, flying fish leaping in and out of the water, rays gliding under the surface, slinky black seals and walruses, circling schools of shiny fish, and enormous whales bellowing to each other. There were hundreds and hundreds of fish, and they were swimming closer and closer to the shore.

"They have come to help us!" cried Hanuman. "They've come to help us build our bridge."

The fish lined up in a row, and floated with their backs showing just above the surface of the water. Hanuman bent down, picked up a small stone and carefully placed it on the back of a fish. The fish floated in the water, carrying the stone on its back!

The monkeys and bears leapt to their feet and began placing stones, rocks and branches on to the fishes' backs. The band worked and worked, until they had built a long, winding path of stepping–stones across the sea. The fish had helped them build a bridge to Lanka.

"Forward, army!" cried Rama, and he blew his conch shell. The band trooped across the bridge and Jambuvan whispered, "Oh, great Creator, ferry us across the sea of life."

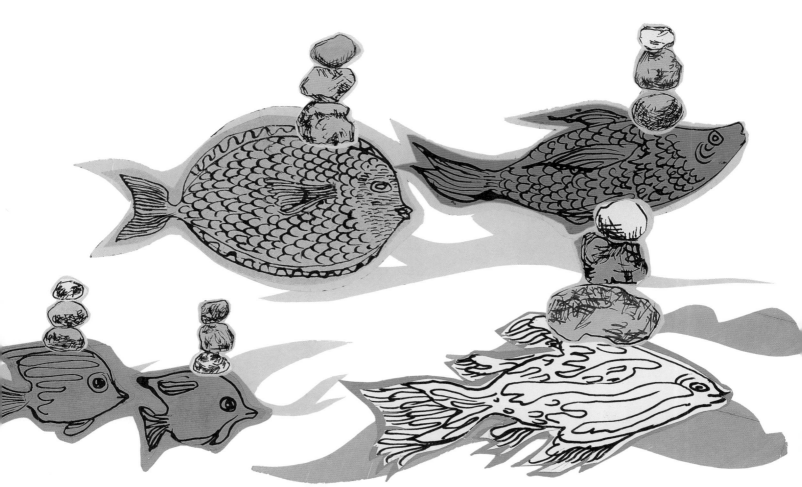

BATTLE BEGINS

Ravana was keeping watch from the highest battlement of his fortress. When he saw Rama and his band arriving on the shores of his kingdom, Ravana buckled on his Invincible Armour – a shining silver breastplate, twenty arm cuffs, and a heavy iron belt which he clasped tightly round his waist.

"Demons!" he commanded. "Arm yourselves and fight."

On one side of the battlefield stood: Slasher, Macerator, Big Belly, Fire–Tongue, Vengeful, Crusher and Man–Destroyer.

On the other side of the battlefield stood: Rama, Lakshman, Hanuman, Jambuvan, the monkeys and the bears.

Ravana surveyed Rama's army and roared with laughter.

"What sort of army do you call that?" sneered Ravana. "A zoo? Go home, Rama. Don't waste your time fighting – you've already lost."

But Rama blew his conch. The sound blasted across the battlefield, and war began.

The demons loosed arrows, hurled spears and wielded knives. Monkeys were slashed. Bears were bashed.

Rama's army fought back. They threw rocks and trees, surrounding the demons, leaping, biting and screaming. The demons used weapons made of fire and poison. Monkeys burst into flames and bears crashed to the ground. But Rama and Lakshman did not give up. They loosed arrow after arrow, striking demons in their chests, piercing demons in their tails.

The battle raged. A monkey lost its fur – Ravana was winning, Rama was losing. A demon was bitten – Rama was winning, Ravana was losing.

The monkeys and bears scaled the walls of the fortress. Bounding and leaping, they stormed the battlements, surging into Ravana's palace. Rama's army raced through the palace, tearing it to pieces. Ravana's army chased after them, but could not stop the destruction. Silver walls crumbled to the ground. Golden doors fell from their hinges.

The palace was covered in smoke.

Ravana looked at the ruins of his palace and said, "Rama is stronger than I thought."

SITA IN THE TOWER

"Take Sita to the tower!" commanded Ravana.

Two demonesses grabbed Sita's wrists and dragged her to a tall tower. The tower was made of iron, with no windows, one steel door, and a massive lock. One demoness pulled a bunch of keys from her pocket and unlocked the steel door. Behind the steel door was another door, made of even thicker steel.

The demonesses cackled, "No one can escape from here!" Rattling the keys, they unlocked the second door, and behind it was another door made of steel.

Sita was terrified. 'No one can save me now,' she thought.

The demonesses unlocked door after door, until they had unlocked seven steel doors. Then they pushed Sita into the tower.

In the gloom, Sita saw golden tables and chairs spread with fruit, clothes and flowers. In the centre of the room stood a great jewelled bed – and Ravana was lying on it!

"All you have to do," he said, "is marry me, and this war will be over."

Sita shook her head. "How many times must I tell you – I am already married."

Ravana shrugged. "Then the war will go on. Rama will die, and so will you." He patted the jewelled bed. "Come here, lie beside me. You might like it."

"I will not share a bed with you," shuddered Sita.

"I am afraid you must," Ravana replied.

Sita walked towards the bed and passed a bowl of flowers. Reaching out, she swiftly pulled a thin blade of grass from the bouquet and whispered to it,

"Mother Earth, help me. Mother Earth, protect me."

Then she sat down on the edge of the bed and laid the blade of grass on the centre of the bed.

Ravana stretched his twenty arms towards her – but was thrown back to the other side of the bed! It was as if there was an invisible wall between them. He snarled and, using all his force, rolled towards Sita. He was thrown back again. There was a powerful force he could not see in the centre of the bed.

Ten heads, twenty arms and all Ravana's magic could not cross a thin blade of grass. Mother Earth protected her daughter, and Sita sat on the other side of the bed, unharmed.

Ravana leapt up from the bed, filled with fury. "When Rama dies," he cried, "you will change your mind." And he stormed out of the tower, leaving Sita alone.

"Oh, please don't die, Rama," cried Sita.

She found a tiny lamp and lit it. Then she held the lamp up in the darkness, and a little flame flickered and glowed. In a small voice, Sita began to sing.

The path is full of darkness.
Show me the way,
show me the way.
Sunlight, moonlight,
starlight, firelight,
show me the way,
show me the way.
But the light that lights the darkest path
is heart–light, self–light.
Let the heart burn bright,
let the self be the light.
Show me the way,
show me the way.

LAKSHMAN WOUNDED

"Rama must die!" roared Ravana. "Fetch my son, Indrajit. He will kill Rama."

A bolt of lightning flashed on to the battlefield, and a demon warrior appeared with shining wings and razor claws. Brilliant light emanated from his body, and he looked, almost, like an angel. Indrajit bowed before Ravana. "Have no fear, Father," he hissed. "I will kill Rama, I will kill Lakshman, I will kill the whole army."

Indrajit pulled a luminous green arrow from his quiver. It was a magic snake-arrow. Indrajit held it in his claws and whispered, "Find. Chase. Destroy."

He fitted the arrow to his bow, took aim and loosed the arrow into the air. The arrow began whizzing and sizzling through the sky like a rocket, scanning and turning this way and that, as if it was looking for something.

Down below on the battlefield, Lakshman was single-handedly fighting eight demons. He spun in a circle, his sword slicing. Lakshman was so gripped by the battle that he did not hear the whirring of the snake-arrow.

The arrow locked on to its target, chased through the air, dived, and destroyed. The arrow pierced Lakshman's heart, and turned into a thousand green, writhing snakes. The snakes wrapped themselves tightly around Lakshman's body and squeezed out all his breath. Lakshman fell to the ground.

A terrible howl went up among the monkeys and the bears.

"Lakshman is dead. Dead."

Rama rushed to his brother's side, and held him close.

"Oh my brother, my dear brother, you made my battle your battle, and now you have died for my sake. I feel as if my own hand has been cut off."

Indrajit laughed, and turned to his father. "This is just the beginning. Leave them to grieve their loss, and to fear who will be next."

HANUMAN LEAPS AGAIN

Lakshman gave a tiny gasp.

"He's alive," whispered Rama, pressing his face close to his brother's. "He's still alive."

Jambuvan stepped forward. "If Lakshman can taste the magic healing herb from the Medicine Mountain before sunrise, he will live."

The King of the Bears turned to Hanuman. "General, you must leap to the Medicine Mountain."

"Not again!" said Hanuman.

"You're a good jumper," said Jambuvan.

"Oh yes, so good, I can leap seventy–three thousand miles to the Himalayas, find the Medicine Mountain, pick the herb, and leap back again – before sunrise! You are joking this time, aren't you?"

"Joking?" said Jambuvan solemnly. "This is a matter of life and death, Hanuman. You have to do it."

Hanuman heard Lakshman's rasping breath.

Jambuvan gazed steadily at Hanuman and said, "Remember who you are, and jump to the Himalayas."

Hanuman looked up at the endless sky. It was getting dark, and the stars were coming out. "I will try," he said.

Hanuman prayed. "Father Wind, help me now." Then he bent his knees, lengthened his tail, opened his arms, and jumped with all his might.

He hurtled through the air. Higher and higher, into the darkening sky, Hanuman flew. Carried by the wind, he leapt over cities and houses with twinkling lights, over dark forests and inky lakes, along rivers gleaming in the moonlight. Swifter than a bird, swifter than thought. Swifter than a hurricane, swifter than a tornado. Swifter than light, swifter than the blink of an eye.

Hanuman flew across the whole of India, until he came to the snowy lands, the icy peaks of the Himalayas. Hanuman circled over the mountains. It was so dark, he could hardly tell one mountain from the next. Then he recognised Mount Everest rising up, a shining blade of ice, towering above the other mountains. He had found Mount Everest – but where was the Medicine Mountain?

THE MEDICINE MOUNTAIN

Hanuman sniffed the air. A sweet and spicy smell was wafting from one of the mountains. He swooped over the mountain and saw herbs poking up out of the snow. The whole mountain was covered in lush, feathery herbs! Hanuman breathed in the smell, and the scent of the magic herbs made him feel stronger.

He landed on the Medicine Mountain and looked about. There were herbs everywhere – many, many different types of herbs.

"There are thousands of herbs here," said Hanuman. "I've no idea which herb will heal Lakshman."

Then Hanuman heard Jambuvan's voice. "Remember who you are, Hanuman."

Hanuman stretched out his arms and they began to grow longer, and longer, and longer. He wrapped his arms around the mountain and began to pull. He pulled, and pulled, and pulled the mountain out of the ground by its roots. He placed the Medicine Mountain in the palm of his hand, and flew up into the air. Hanuman flew back to Lanka, carrying the whole mountain!

As Hanuman hurtled through the air, it began to get light. The sun was rising! "Surya," cried Hanuman, "you can't rise yet. You can't rise until Lakshman is healed." Hanuman grabbed the sun, squashed it under his arm, and the sky went dark!

Hanuman flew. Swifter than a bird, swifter than thought. Swifter than a hurricane, swifter than a tornado. Swifter than light, swifter than the blink of an eye. Hanuman flew with the sun under his arm and the mountain in the palm of his hand.

At last he saw the shores of Lanka, and swooped down, placing the mountain on the edge of the battlefield. "I didn't know which herb to pick," he said. "So I brought the whole mountain."

The monkeys and bears cheered.

But Hanuman muttered, "Get Jambuvan. And tell him to hurry, I'm feeling rather hot."

Jambuvan sniffed the mountain with his large black nose, until he came to a small delicate plant. "That's the one," he cried.

Jambuvan picked the herb and held it under Lakshman's nostrils. The bear gently squeezed the plant's tender leaves with his huge paws and a drop of sap fell on to Lakshman's lips. Lakshman gulped in air. The green snakes wriggled loose, unwound and slithered away. Lakshman opened his eyes, and the magic arrow fell from his chest. Then he sat up, looked about, and smiled.

Rama threw his arms around his brother's neck and hugged him.

At last, Hanuman lifted his arm and Surya, the sun, shot up into the sky. Dawn broke, and Surya's voice boomed across the sky.

"Hanuman, Monkey General, you tried to catch me when you were little…"

"DON'T CALL ME LITTLE!" Hanuman shouted at the sun.

"Forgive me," cried Surya. "You tried to catch me when you were…a boy. I knew then that you were special. But I did not think you would try to catch me again – and succeed! May the stories of your courage and adventures be told for all eternity."

"Thank you," said Hanuman, and he bowed.

And Surya soared up into the sky, filling the world with light.

GRIEF AND FURY

Lakshman picked up the magic snake–arrow and fitted it to his bow.

"Find. Chase. Destroy," he whispered, and the arrow whistled into the sky. Whizzing and sizzling, scanning and turning, the arrow began looking for someone.

At the banqueting table, Indrajit was celebrating his victory. He was feasting, piling his plate with mounds of rice and ladles of spicy curry. He did not hear the whirring of the snake–arrow as it found its target, chased, dived, and destroyed. The arrow pierced Indrajit's heart and wrapped him in a thousand snakes. Indrajit slumped in his chair, dead.

Ravana rushed to his son's side. He lifted Indrajit into his arms and wept.

"Oh my son, my dear son, you made my battle your battle, and now you have died for my sake. I feel as if my own hand has been cut off."

Ravana stayed by the body all day and all night. Then, as dawn broke on the following day, he bellowed across the battlefield, "It's one on one, Rama – you against ME!"

Ravana's army beat the drums for war, and Rama's army took their places on the field. Rama lifted his conch, but before he could blow it, the sky went dark. The battlefield turned pitch black. Ravana had already begun to fight.

"Ravana's not using ordinary weapons, he's using magic ones," Lakshman shouted into the darkness. "Use astras."

Rama pulled an astra from his quiver. It looked like a silver, shining arrow, but it had magical powers. He fitted the astra to his bow, aimed it into the dark sky and let it fly. The powerful astra shattered the darkness with a flash, filling the battlefield with light.

Ravana launched an astra of flames. Fire crackled, racing across the field, setting the monkeys' fur alight.

Then Rama hurled an astra of water. Rain pelted the ground, putting out the flames, and the field was left damp and smoking.

There was a roar, and Ravana appeared in the centre of the battlefield,

each of his twenty hands holding a curved sword. There was a second roar, and another Ravana appeared on the edge of the field. There was a third roar, and another Ravana appeared at the back of the field. A fourth… a fifth… the battlefield was filled with Ravanas. There was a whole army of Ravanas. There were Ravanas everywhere – like an endless set of mirrors reflecting for eternity. There were thousands and thousands of Ravanas!

"HO! HO! HO!" boomed all the Ravanas. "COME AND GET ME, RAMA."

"Don't be afraid, Rama," shouted Lakshman. "Ravana is using the astra of illusion. Use the astra of perception."

Rama stood firm and stilled his mind until his thoughts were fine and sharp. Then he used his thought like a weapon. His perception cut through the illusion like a knife. He could see what was real and what was disguise. The thousand Ravanas vanished, leaving only one Ravana, standing alone.

Rama and Ravana faced each other on the battlefield.

RAVANA'S DEATH

Rama drew his sword and swiftly cut off one of Ravana's heads. The head fell to the ground, but instantly another head grew in its place. Rama sliced at Ravana's neck again and a second head fell to the ground. But another sprang up in its place. Ravana slashed the air with his twenty swords, cutting and hacking wildly at Rama, until Rama was covered in blood.

Lakshman watched in horror. "Ravana is indestructible," he cried.

Jambuvan shook his great head. "Ravana's death must be hidden in his body," he said. "Think! Where could his death hide?"

"Somewhere secret," said Lakshman. "Somewhere he is careful of..."

"What about that iron belt?" asked Jambuvan. "He could be protecting something under there."

"His belly button?" said Lakshman.

"Of course!" cried Jambuvan. "No one would think to kill him there."

Lakshman shouted as loudly as he could. "Ravana's death is hidden in his belly button!"

Rama heard Lakshman cry, and slipped his sword up and under the iron belt. He stabbed Ravana hard and deep through the centre of his navel. The sword went into Ravana's belly button, and did not stop – it went through Ravana's stomach, and came out the other side.

Ravana gave a mighty groan and tumbled to the ground. His twenty arms went limp, his twenty eyes rolled back in their sockets, and his ten heads sank on to his chest. Ravana was dead.

The battlefield fell silent. The demon army stared in disbelief. A few demons shouted, "The King is dead!" But their cries faded, and they began to shiver and shrink with terror. One by one the demons started running, scuttling under rocks and stones, disappearing into caves, fleeing underground, never to be seen again.

Rama knelt by Ravana's body, and pressed his hands together in prayer. His voice echoed in the stillness.

"No more war, no more fame, no more victory, no more joy, now Ravana is dead. He was a great king, but the time of the demons is over."

SITA IN FLAMES

"War is over!" cried Rama. "Find Sita."

The monkeys and bears ran through the ruins of the palace, leaping over crumbled golden walls, scrambling through piles of silver rubble, calling for Sita.

They came to the iron tower, but its seven steel doors were locked and bolted. At once, Hanuman began to grow. Bigger, and bigger, and bigger. He grew to the size of a normal monkey. He grew to the size of a king monkey. He grew to the size of a human being. He grew to the size of an elephant.

Then he charged towards the door, hurling himself against it with all his might. The steel lock cracked and the steel door crumpled to the ground. Behind it was another door. Hanuman hurled himself at the second door, smashing through door after door, until seven steel doors and seven steel locks lay broken and bent on the ground.

Standing in the darkness was Sita, shining like a bright flame. Hanuman felt his heart leap. He threw his arms around her. "Oh, lovely Sita!" he said. "I am so happy to see you."

Sita smiled and stroked his furry head.

Then Rama and Lakshman rushed into the tower. Rama opened his arms to embrace his wife, and suddenly saw the great jewelled bed in the centre of the room. He stopped and stared at it, and his heart was filled with dark jealousy.

"Did you share this bed with Ravana?" he asked.

The monkeys and bears fell silent.

Sita held out her hand towards her husband. "The Demon King made me," she said.

Rama pushed her aside. "You shared a bed with another man!" he shouted.

"Rama, I was his prisoner. But look!" Sita lifted the blade of grass from the centre of the bed. "Mother Earth protected me – Ravana never crossed this line."

Rama shook his head. "I cannot have a wife who has shared a bed with another man."

Sita stared at Rama in disbelief. "Do you think I betrayed you? If you think that, then you are not a true warrior. I am innocent. War has made you lose your mind. You have forgotten who I am. And you have forgotten yourself."

Sita turned to Lakshman. "Build a fire," she commanded. "Build a fire at once, on this very spot. If I have done anything wrong – may the fire burn me."

Lakshman turned to his brother, horrified. "Rama, you must stop this nonsense. We did not fight the war for this."

But Rama growled, "Build a fire."

Tears poured down Lakshman's face as he made a pile of broken furniture. "This is not peace," he said, lighting the fire.

Sita bowed before the flames.

"*Om Agni swaha*," she prayed. "Agni, God of Fire, I salute you. Know I am faithful, know my heart is true." Then she stepped into the flames. The fire burned brightly. The flames licked at Sita's dress, crackled around her bare feet and swept up her body. Fire engulfed her, but the flames did not touch her, the flames did not burn her.

The fire began to glitter and dance. The flames looked like a tiger, an eye, a hand, a mouth. The fiery hand rested on Sita's heart, and the fiery mouth said, "I cannot burn what is pure. Earth and gold never burn. And so it is with Sita."

Sita walked through the flames unharmed. Not a thread of her dress caught fire. And as she walked, the flames turned to flowers. Flowers! Sita stood in a heap of sweet, red flowers.

Rama hung his head and began to cry. "Oh, Sita! The fire was in me. Exile. Loss. War. Death. I had forgotten that love is stronger than all these things."

Rama knelt at Sita's feet and placed his hand over his heart. "A true warrior asks for forgiveness," he said.

Sita knelt beside him. "War and death will continue for ever," she replied, "unless we can find it in our hearts to forgive."

And Rama and Sita knelt, weeping and laughing, wiping away tears and wiping away pain.

A PATH OF FLAMES

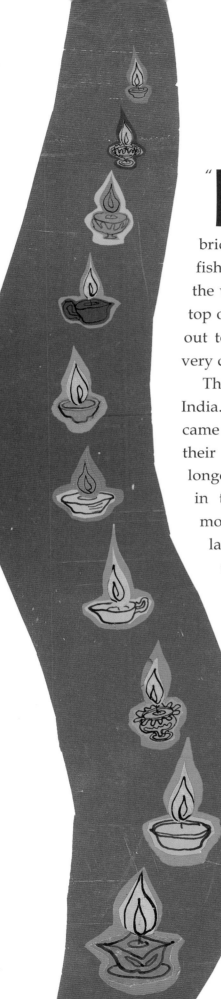

"Let's go home!" cried Lakshman.

The band set off, with General Hanuman in front. Everyone sang as they crossed the bridge, and when they reached the other side the fish swam away and the bridge sank down under the waves. Some of the rocks and stones fell on top of each other, leaving a trail of rocks jutting out towards Lanka which is still there to this very day.

The band continued northwards, across India. It grew dark and, one by one, people came out of their houses and put lamps on their doorsteps to light the way. People no longer feared demons and no longer hid in their homes in darkness. More and more people lit lamps, placing gleaming lanterns, flickering candles and burning torches to light the path.

The flames shone in the darkness and the band followed the trail of lights. On the way, Rama and Sita said goodbye to the bears and the monkeys, but Hanuman continued on the journey with them. And the shimmering path of flames stretched ahead, glittering and dancing into the distance – a path of flames leading them home.

KING RAMA

Rama's brothers, Bharata and Shatrughna, rushed to greet them. Bharata took Rama's hand and led him to the throne. Rama's sandals were still there, exactly where Bharata had put them.

"Your sandals have been waiting for you all this time," said Bharata. "Now you will be king." And he bent and placed the sandals on his brother's feet.

Rama looked around. Everything had changed. There was no more dispute. The time of the demons really had come to an end. And at last Rama was crowned King, and Sita his Queen.

Sita took her golden necklace and hung it around Hanuman's neck.

"How can I ever thank you, my little monkey?" she asked.

Hanuman felt so happy – for once he didn't mind being little, as Sita's little monkey was just what he wanted to be!

"Don't send me away," he said. "I want to stay with you for ever."

So Hanuman stayed with Rama and Sita, in their kingdom, protected by love.

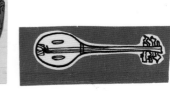

EARTH TO HEAVEN

Garuda, King of the Birds, landed before Rama's throne.

"I have come to take you home," he said.

"Home?" laughed Rama. "But I am home!"

"Your job is done, Vishnu," said Garuda.

"What do you mean? Why are you calling me Vishnu? I am Rama and this is my wife Sita."

"Remember who you are," said the great bird. "You are gods. Rama, you are really Vishnu – God of Protection. Sita, you are really Lakshmi – Goddess of Love. You came down to Earth to stop the demons. Your job is done, and now it is time to return to Heaven."

"But I don't want to leave," cried Rama. "I love Earth, even with all its pain and suffering. A short life on Earth is sweeter than an eternity in Heaven."

Even as Rama spoke, he was beginning to remember who he really was. And his earthly form began to fade.

"It is time to leave, Vishnu," said Garuda, spreading his golden wings.

And the gods Vishnu and Lakshmi climbed on to Garuda's back, and the bird soared up into the sky, through blue Heaven.

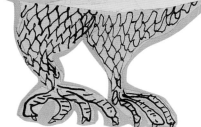

THE MONKEY AGAIN

"But what about you, Hanuman?" I said to the monkey sitting above my desk. "What about you? Sita promised that you would be by her side for ever."

"Oh, but I'm always by her side," said the monkey. "Whenever the story of Rama and Sita is told, I'm there, listening. I am the first to arrive, and the last to leave. And as Surya gave me the gift of immortal life, I will be listening to the story for ever."

"So who will tell the story next?" I asked.

"I don't know," said the monkey. "But I do know that wherever it is, I will be there."

"Now I shall perform
what the Gods and the World,
the moving and the still,
shall keep narrating
so long as Earth endures."
(A way of starting Ramayana, North India.)

There are hundreds and hundreds of different versions of the story of Rama and Sita. The story has been performed throughout India and south–east Asia for at least 2000 years.

It was first written down in about 400 AD by the Indian poet Valmiki. He collected stories and songs connected with Rama and Sita and wrote them down as the epic *Ramayana*. There are countless other versions, among them the 11th century Tamil version by Kamban which was etched on palm leaves, and the 16th century *Ramacharitamanasa* by the north–Indian poet Tulsi Das.

The story has crossed seas and mountains, languages and religions. There are Muslim versions in Java, and Buddhist versions in Thailand. The story exists as shadow plays in Indonesia, as temple carvings in Cambodia, and as dances throughout India.

The *Ramayana* has travelled far and wide, with each storyteller re-making the story for their audience. It is still being told today, and some of these versions have not been written down yet. So *Ramayana* is a narrative with no ending. But sometimes when the story is told, the storyteller will spread a white cloth on the ground, so that Hanuman can come and sit on the cloth, and listen.

Here are some versions that have inspired me:

The Monkey God and other Hindu Tales
Debjani Chatterjee. Rupa Paperback. 1993.
This is a very readable, lively and faithful retelling.

Ramayana, King Rama's way:Valmiki's Ramayana told in English prose.
William Buck. University of California Press. 1976.
An accurate and beautifully told translation. The text includes many of the
sub–stories and gives the feel of the dynamic, interlaced storytelling style that
is the *Ramayana.*

The Ramayana
R. K. Narayan. Vision Books 1987.
A famous Indian author's loving retelling.

Hanuman: an introduction
Devdutt Pattanaik. Valkis, Feffer and Simons Ltd. 2001
The life of Hanuman in images, stories and poems.

Many Ramayanas. The diversity of a narrative tradition in South East Asia
Edited by Paula Richman. University of California Press. 1991.
The fluid relationship between written and performed versions of *Ramayana*
has been documented in these excellent collections of essays.

Making Versions: a storytelling journey with Ramayana by *Sally Pomme*
Clayton, in **Story: the heart of the matter.**
Edited by Maggie Butt. Greenwich Exchange Publishing. 2007.

"Both teller and listener
shall be treasurers of wisdom
for Rama's tale is mysterious."

Indian saying

Thank you to The Unicorn Theatre and all those who helped
me create my version: Tony Graham; Ajit Pandaye;
Sukhdev Mishra; Shyan; Rick Wilson; Richard Aylwin;
Amina Khayyam; Helen East; Katinka Haycraft.
And to Linzie for sharing Sri Lanka with me.